# Wizard Crystal

# Wizard Crystal

By Manus Pinkwater

Dodd, Mead & Company, New York

ISBN: 0-396-06704-2
Library of Congress Catalog Card Number: 72-5946
Printed in the United States of America

*For Lucile Potts*

THERE were some frogs in a pond. All the frogs were happy. There was enough to eat. There were logs and lily pads to sit on. No danger ever came to that pond.

At night the frogs would sing. Their voices carried over the smooth water:

*GUNK* this pond, *GUNK* this pond,
*GAGUNK* warm sun, *GAGUNK* warm sun,
*GUNK* bright stars, *GUNK* bright stars,
*GAGUNK* safe home, *GAGUNK* safe home,
*GUNK* happy place, *GUNK* happy place.

In the pond, at the very bottom, was a magic crystal. The frogs did not know it was magic, but they liked it very much. It made them happy to swim down and see the crystal shining and sparkling. It made them happy to take care of the crystal and keep it free of weeds and moss. It made them happy just to think about their wonderful crystal.

There was a wizard living near. He had been sitting in one place for 102 years reading a book of magic. It was a hard book full of secrets. The wizard was looking for the secret of being happy. He had been unhappy every day for 307 years and he was tired of it.

One day he read in a book about a magic crystal. He read that whoever has the crystal will always be happy, so the wizard made up his mind that he would find it.

To find the crystal was not easy. The book did not say where it was. The wizard built a sort of magic compass to find the crystal. A compass points North, but this one pointed to the crystal.

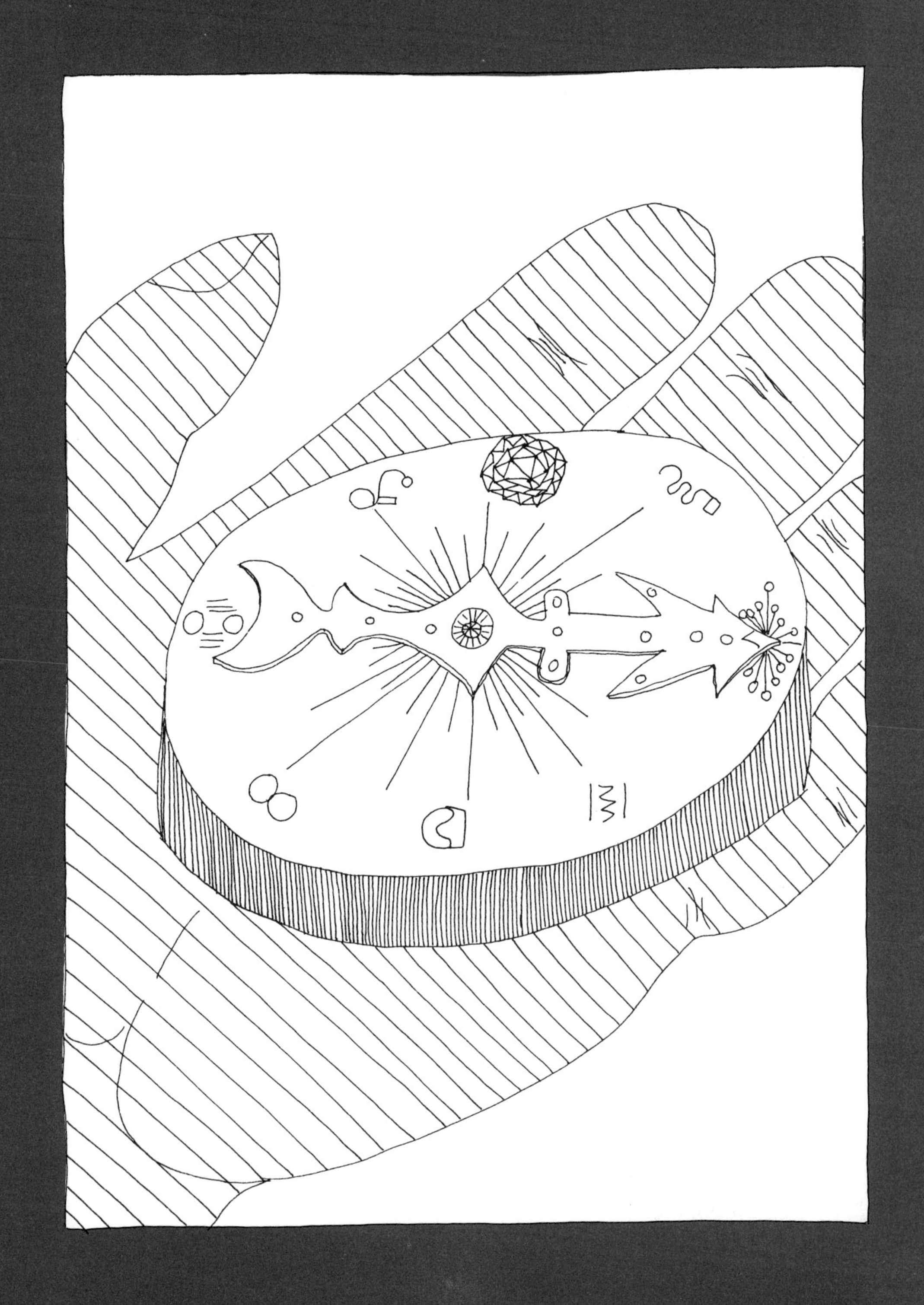

With the magic compass, the wizard started through the forest searching for the crystal. The needle of the compass pointed to the crystal and the wizard walked in that direction.

Because he was looking at the compass while he walked, the wizard bumped into a lot of trees and fell in some holes in the forest. When he came to the frog pond he fell in that too.

The wizard walked around the pond, and as he walked the needle moved, always pointing to the middle of the pond. Then the wizard knew that the crystal was there.

With a long-handled net the wizard scooped out the crystal on the first try. "How easy it is to get the thing which will make you happy!" he thought.

When the frogs saw this, they started after the wizard to get their crystal back, but frogs are slow and wizards are fast.

When the frogs reached the wizard's house, it was night and he was inside with the door locked.

Through the locked window the frogs could see the crystal shining on the table and the wizard asleep. He was dreaming of being happy always.

The frogs did not know what to do. They sat in a circle around the wizard's house and sang a song to help themselves think.

*GUNK* think hard! *GUNK* think hard!
*GAGUNK* what to do, *GAGUNK* what to do,
*GUNK* think hard! *GUNK* think hard!

They sang of their home in the pond. They sang of the sun and the stars. They sang all through the night. The wizard never woke up, but he heard the songs in his sleep and dreamed of frogs and stars and lily pads.

And while the frogs sang and the wizard dreamed, magic happened. The place in the forest changed. The house of the wizard changed. The wizard changed.

The crystal shone brighter than ever before.

Morning came. When the wizard woke up he was not unhappy any more. He was not a wizard any more either. He was a frog. The house was gone. In its place in the forest was a pond.

In that pond all the frogs were happy. There was enough to eat. There were logs and lily pads to sit on. No danger ever came to that pond. At night the frogs would sing:

*GUNK* this pond, *GUNK* this pond,
*GAGUNK* warm sun, *GAGUNK* warm sun,
*GUNK* bright stars, *GUNK* bright stars,
*GAGUNK* safe home, *GAGUNK* safe home,
*GUNK* happy place, *GUNK* happy place.

Gr.1-3
J
Pinkwater, M.
Wizard crystal.
3.95 Gr.1-3
Cranford Public Library
224 Walnut Avenue
Cranford, New Jersey 07016
Tel. 276-1826